For Marius Jr.
—M.M.-K.

For my parents, with love and gratitude
—V.G.

www.goldenbooks.com
www.randomhouse.com/kids
Library of Congress Control Number: 2007902084
ISBN: 978-0-375-84799-8
MANUFACTURED IN CHINA
10 9 8 7 6 5 4 3 2 1
First Edition

# A Scent-sational Valentine

By Mary Man-Kong  Illustrated by Viviana Garofoli

A GOLDEN BOOK • NEW YORK

It's almost Valentine's Day! Sammy has a secret crush on one of his classmates, Allie—but he's too shy to tell her.

"Why don't you give Allie something special to show her how you feel?" Sammy's dad suggests.

"That's a great idea!" exclaims Sammy. "In fact, I'll give her something super-special every day until Valentine's Day!"

On Monday, Sammy leaves a box of candies for Allie.
"*Mmm!* I love cinnamon!" Allie exclaims. "I wonder who left these for me?"

Can you smell the cinnamon?

"What should I give Allie next?" Sammy asks his best friend, Katie.
"Let's go to the flower shop," Katie suggests.

"How about this Venus flytrap?" asks Sammy.
"I'm not sure Allie will like that," says Katie.

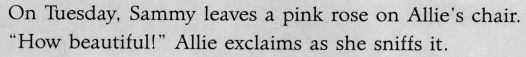

On Tuesday, Sammy leaves a pink rose on Allie's chair.
"How beautiful!" Allie exclaims as she sniffs it.

**Can you smell the rose?**

During his walk home from school, Sammy stops by
the candy store with his friend Gus.

"How about these jelly worms for Allie?" Sammy asks.

"Those are awesome!" exclaims Gus. "But I'm not sure
Allie will like them. . . ."

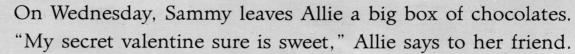

On Wednesday, Sammy leaves Allie a big box of chocolates.
"My secret valentine sure is sweet," Allie says to her friend.

Can you smell the chocolate?

That afternoon, Sammy goes with his mother to a department store. "Vampire robots!" exclaims Sammy. "This will be a great gift for Allie."

"Those are nice," says his mom. "But maybe you should get Allie something else?"

On Thursday, Sammy leaves Allie a bottle of perfume. "How heavenly!" exclaims Allie. "My secret valentine sure has good taste—and a great sense of smell!"

# Can you smell the perfume?

After school, Sammy and his dad stop at the grocery store.

"Look!" exclaims Sammy. "Sour pickles! Do you think Allie would like one?"

"Hmm, maybe we should get Allie something sweet instead," suggests his dad.

On Friday, Sammy leaves a heart-shaped
cookie on Allie's desk with a little note.
"Strawberry is my favorite!" cries Allie.
"And I can't wait to meet my secret valentine."

Allie,
Please meet me
at the Pizza Palace
on Saturday
at 1 o'clock.
Your Secret
Valentine

Can you smell the strawberry cookie?

On Saturday, Sammy goes to the Pizza Palace, but he still doesn't know how to tell Allie how much he likes her.

"I'm so nervous," Sammy says to his dad. "I don't know what to say."

"Don't worry, Sammy," says his dad. "I'm sure you'll find a way to tell her."

"I've got it!" Sammy exclaims.

When Allie and her parents walk in, Sammy has a special surprise just for her. "Happy Valentine's Day, Allie!"

"Pepperoni?" Allie asks with a smile. "My favorite! You are the best secret valentine ever!"

Can you smell the pizza?

BE MY VALENTINE

Happy Valentine's Day!